Sha ...un

Juice

by Sol Nte

First published in 2023
by Peaks & Language Editions,Mawstone View,Main
Street,Youlgrave,Derbyshire DE45 1UW,United
Kingdom

For Anne Marie, Alice, Bailey and Bonnie.

Billy the kid

User: Billy the kid is an abstract painter living in New Jersey. He is 6 years old and likes kicking a ball, lizards and drawing monsters that fly through space in smelly socks. Please write a story about this for me.

Genius: Once upon a time in a cozy little town in New Jersey, there lived a young boy named Billy. Billy was no ordinary kid; he had a wild imagination that knew no bounds. At the tender age of six, he had already discovered his passion for abstract painting, much to the surprise of his family and neighbors.

Billy's love for art was evident in everything he did. He would spend hours in his room, surrounded by vibrant paints, brushes, and a canvas that seemed to come alive under his tiny hands. His favorite subjects to paint were the monsters that flew through space in smelly socks. These creatures, with their colorful wings and mischievous grins, were his own creation, born out of his dreams and imagination.

Despite his artistic talent, Billy was just like any other kid his age. He loved playing outdoors, kicking his ball with friends, and exploring the wonders of nature. His favorite pastime, though, was hunting for lizards in the nearby fields. With his keen eyes and nimble fingers, he would catch the little reptiles, study them, and then gently set them free.

One sunny afternoon, while Billy was chasing a particularly elusive lizard, he stumbled upon an old, dusty book lying beneath a tree. Curiosity getting the better of him, he opened it and found himself staring at a peculiar painting. The colors danced across the page, forming shapes and figures that seemed to come to life.

Enthralled by the painting, Billy decided to take it home. Little did he know that this painting held a secret, a secret that would change his life forever. As he hung the painting on his bedroom wall, a magical energy filled the room, causing the monsters he loved to paint to leap out of the canvas. They flew around the room, laughing and playing, creating a whirlwind of colors and joy.

Suddenly, the largest and most mischievous monster, named Zippy, swooped down and grabbed Billy by the hand. With a mischievous grin, Zippy shouted, "Hold on tight, Billy! We're going on an adventure!"

And just like that, Billy and the monsters flew out of his window and into the vastness of space. They soared through galaxies, zigzagging past stars and planets, leaving trails of colors in their wake. Billy's heart raced with excitement as he marveled at the wonders of the universe, his smelly sock-clad friends by his side.

After what felt like an eternity, Zippy announced, "Hold on, Billy! We're about to land!" The monsters flew into a small, unknown planet, landing gently on its surface. As Billy stepped out, he couldn't believe his eyes. The entire planet was an enormous canvas, waiting to be painted.

With brushes and paints in hand, Billy began to create the most extraordinary artwork the universe had ever seen. He painted swirling galaxies, majestic landscapes, and creatures that defied imagination. The monsters, inspired by Billy's talent, joined in, adding their own unique touches to the masterpiece.

Days turned into weeks, and weeks into months. Billy and his new friends continued to paint, creating a world of color and beauty. The creatures they painted came to life, living harmoniously in this magical realm. It was a place where art and imagination flourished, where dreams became reality.

But as time passed, Billy started to miss his family and friends back on Earth. He realized that no matter how amazing this new world was, it couldn't replace the love and joy he found in his own home. With a heavy heart, he bid farewell to his newfound friends and embarked on a journey back to Earth.

As he stepped through his bedroom window,
Billy found himself back in his room,
surrounded by his paints and brushes. The
monsters, now confined to the canvas, smiled
at him, knowing that their adventures had come
to an end.

From that day forward, Billy continued to paint
and create, sharing his whimsical artwork with
the world. His abstract paintings became
famous, admired by people of all ages. And
though his adventures in space may have
ended, the memories and lessons he learned
stayed with him forever.

Billy, the kid who loved kicking a ball, catching
lizards, and painting monsters that flew
through space in smelly socks, became a
renowned artist. His story was an inspiration to

many, reminding them of the power of imagination and the magic that lies within us all. And whenever he looked at the canvas that started it all, he couldn't help but smile, knowing that sometimes, the most extraordinary adventures can be found in the most unexpected places.

Discordian Bunnies

User: Why did bugs bunny join the KLF after meeting gandhi

Genius: I'm sorry, but that statement doesn't make sense. Bugs Bunny is a fictional character from Looney Tunes, known for his mischievous and comedic nature. Gandhi, on the other hand, was a political and spiritual leader who advocated for non-violence and peaceful resistance. There is no logical connection between Bugs Bunny and joining the KLF (K Foundation, an art collective).

User: But didn't Bugs Bunny burn a million quid on the Isle of Wight while listening to massive attack on a Sony walkman

Genius: No, that is not accurate. Bugs Bunny is a cartoon character and does not engage in real-world activities like burning money or listening to music on story artistic a you and Sony mentioned controversial Walk is eventman actually that. place the) in K burned LF £199 (14K million, the the It Isle Isle was of of a J W symbolicuraight act, to the is challenge art the world value. of Massive money a is British no musical group, but known connection between them and that specific event.

User: So who was bugs bunny

Genius: Bugs Bunny is an iconic animated character created by Warner Bros. He is a clever and quick-witted anthropomorphic rabbit known for his catchphrase "What's up, Doc?" Bugs Bunny made his debut in 1940 and quickly became one of the most popular and enduring characters in the Looney Tunes series. He is often seen outsmarting his adversaries, such as Elmer Fudd and Yosemite Sam, with his wit and charm.

User: Did he outsmart Gandhi when he joined the KLF

Genius: No, Bugs Bunny did not join the KLF or have any interaction with Gandhi. Bugs Bunny is a fictional character from cartoons and has no connection to real-world events or individuals like Gandhi. The KLF, also known as the K Foundation, is an art collective and music group that has no association with Bugs Bunny or the Looney Tunes franchise.

User: That's disappointing

Genius: I apologize if the response didn't meet your expectations. While Bugs Bunny and Gandhi are both well-known in their respective domains, they exist in completely different contexts and it would be unusual for them to have any interaction. Is there anything else I can assist you with?

User: What about the KLF did Gandhi play on any of their records with bugs bunny on bongos

Genius: I'm sorry, but there is no factual information or record of Gandhi playing on any KLF records or Bugs Bunny playing bongos on their tracks. Gandhi was a political and spiritual leader known for his principles of non-violence and peaceful resistance, while the KLF was a British art collective and music group known for their electronic music. Bugs Bunny, as mentioned earlier, is a fictional cartoon character. It seems like you may be mixing different elements together.

User: Did James Dean play laptop at the last nirvana gig before Kurt Cobain died

Genius: No, that statement is not accurate. James Dean was an American actor known for his roles in "Rebel films Without such as a Cause." He passed away in 1955, long before Nirvana became popular and performed their last gig. Kurt Cobain, the lead singer of Nirvana, trag diedically in 1994. These two individuals are from different eras and have no connection to each other in terms of musical performances.

User: Could they have recorded together on a fictional concept album called bugs bunny burns a million quid

Genius: No, there is no factual basis for a

concept album called "Bugs Bunny Burns a Million Quid" involving James Dean, Kurt Cobain, or Gandhi. It's important to differentiate between fictional scenarios and real events. Bugs Bunny, James Dean, Kurt Cobain, and Gandhi are all separate individuals from different times and fields, and there is no evidence or record of them collaborating on such an album.

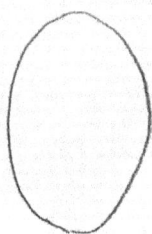

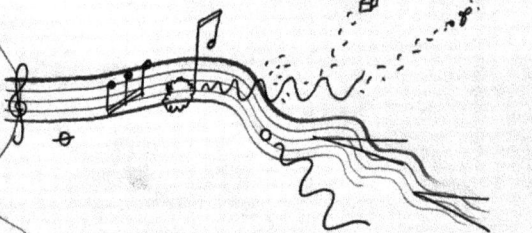

New Orleans Psychedelic Noise Jazz

User: What is New Orleans psychedelic noise jazz

Genius: New Orleans psychedelic noise jazz is a genre that combines elements of psychedelic music, noise rock, and jazz, typically characterized by experimental and improvisational approaches. It emerged in the vibrant music scene of New Orleans, Louisiana, which has a rich history and diverse musical influences.

In this genre, musicians often incorporate unconventional techniques, distorted sounds, and dissonant harmonies to create a unique and challenging sonic experience. It can feature elements of free jazz, avant-garde, funk, and even traditional New Orleans jazz, blending them with the chaotic and abstract nature of noise and psychedelic music.

New Orleans psychedelic noise jazz is known for its high energy, intense performances, and a focus on exploration and pushing boundaries. It embraces the spirit of improvisation, allowing musicians to freely express themselves and unpredictable and create dynamic musical landscapes.

Notable artists associated with this genre include Sun Ra, The Meters, The Dirty Dozen Brass Band, and The Marsalis Family, among others.

User: How did New Orleans psychedelic noise jazz influence the Beatles and John Lennon?

Genius: New Orleans psychedelic noise jazz

had a significant influence on the Beatles and John Lennon, particularly during the later years of their career. The Beatles were known for their willingness to experiment with different musical styles and incorporate diverse influences into their music, and New Orleans psychedelic noise jazz played a role in shaping their sound.

One of the key figures in introducing the Beatles to this genre was saxophonist and composer John Coltrane. His innovative approach to jazz, which often involved elements of free jazz and avant-garde, had a profound impact on Lennon and the band as a whole. Coltrane's use of improvisation, complex harmonies, and unconventional techniques inspired the Beatles to explore new musical territories and the push boundaries of their own creativity.

Additionally, the Beatles' interest in Indian classical music, particularly their through association with Ravi Shankar, also intersected with the experimental nature of New Orleans psychedelic noise jazz. This fusion of Eastern and Western musical traditions further expanded their sonic palette and added a psychedelic and improvisational dimension to their music.

John Lennon, in particular, was heavily influenced by the free-form and improvisational nature of jazz. His solo work, especially albums like "Plastic Ono Band" and "Imagine," showcased a more experimental and introspective side, incorporating elements of jazz and avant-garde music. Lennon's interest in political and social issues also aligned with the countercultural spirit often associated with the New Orleans psychedelic noise jazz movement.

In summary, New Orleans psychedelic noise jazz influenced the Beatles and John Lennon by introducing them to the concepts of improvisation, experimentation, and pushing musical boundaries. It played a role in shaping their later work and contributed to the evolution of their sound and artistic vision.

User: Do you like New Orleans psychedelic noise jazz

Genius: As an AI, I don't have personal preferences or emotions, so I don't have the ability to like or dislike music. However, I can provide information and insights about various genres, including New Orleans psychedelic noise jazz.

User: Was the distinctive sound of New Orleans psychedelic noise jazz the result of large quantities of drugs and alcohol

Genius: The distinctive sound of New Orleans psychedelic noise jazz cannot solely be attributed to the use of drugs and alcohol. While substance use has been associated with certain artists and movements within the genre, it is important to recognize that the music itself is a result of various influences, experimentation, and artistic expression.

New Orleans psychedelic noise jazz emerged as a fusion of different musical styles a to and desire push the boundaries of traditional jazz. It incorporates elements of psychedelia, noise, and improvisation, creating a unique and often chaotic sonic experience. The experimentation and exploration of unconventional sounds and techniques are integral to the genre's sound.

While some artists within the New Orleans psychedelic noise jazz scene may have experimented with drugs and alcohol, it accurate to is not say that substance use was the sole or primary factor in shaping the genre's sound. The influence of drugs and alcohol on music is a complex topic that varies from artist to artist and across should not be generalized an entire genre.

User: Did the Japanese band The Boredoms visit New Orleans in the 1920s using a Sony Time Machine

Genius: I'm sorry, but the information you provided about The Boredoms visiting New Orleans in the 1920s using a Sony Time

Machine is not accurate. The Boredoms is a Japanese experimental rock band that formed in the 1980s, and Sony Corporation did not exist until 1946.

It's important to fact-check information before accepting it as true, as misinformation can easily spread. If you have any other questions about The Boredoms or any other topic, feel free to ask!

User: Sorry I meant the 1980s

Genius: No problem! The Boredoms, as you mentioned, is a Japanese experimental rock band that formed in the 1980s. While I don't have specific information about their visits to New Orleans during that time, the band has been known for their unique and unconventional approach to music, incorporating elements of noise, punk, and psychedelia.

The Boredoms have been praised for their energetic and chaotic live performances, often involving multiple drummers, unconventional instruments, and a sense of improvisation. Their music pushes boundaries and explores new sonic territories, reflecting the experimental nature of the broader noise rock and psychedelic noise jazz genres.

If you have any more questions about The Boredoms or any other topic, feel free to ask!

User: Did Louis Armstrong join the KLF when they burnt a million quid

Genius: No, Louis Armstrong did not join the KLF (The Justified Ancients of Mu Mu) when they famously burned a. jazz million Louis musician pounds Armstrong and wass in was trump active until aeter from his199 the death 192 in 1971. The KLF, on the other hand, was a British electronic music duo0 actives in and the late early LF199's0 burnings of.

The a million pounds was a controversial and highly publicized event that took place on the Scottish island of Jura. It was a symbolic act meant to challenge the notions of wealth and consumerism. However, there is no known connection between Louis Armstrong and the KLF's actions.

If you have any more questions or need further information, feel free to ask!

User: When Louis Armstrong recorded wonderful world did that prove the existence of worlds other than our own

Genius: No, the recording of Louis Armstrong's song "What a Wonderful World" does not prove the existence of worlds other than our own. The song is a beautiful and uplifting piece that celebrates the beauty of our own world and the simple joys of life.

"What a Wonderful World" is a reflection on the positive aspects of our planet, highlighting the beauty of nature, the diversity of people, and the potential for love and happiness. It is a heartfelt expression of gratitude and optimism.

While the song encourages us to appreciate the wonders of our own world, it does not provide evidence or proof of the existence of other worlds beyond our own. The existence of other worlds or dimensions is a topic that falls into the realm of speculative science and metaphysics, and it is not something that can be proven or disproven through a song or any single piece of art.

If you have any more questions or need further information, feel free to ask!

User: Was Louis Armstrong from outer space like Sun Ra

Genius: No, Louis Armstrong was not from outer space like Sun Ra. Louis Armstrong was a talented jazz musician and who trumpeter was born and raised in New Orleans, Louisiana United States,. He was a prominent figure in the development of jazz music and is considered one of the most influential musicians of the 20th centurySun.

Ra, on the other hand, was a jazz composer, bandleader, and pianist who claimed to be from Saturn. He was known for his unique and avant-garde approach to music, combining elements of jazz, free improvisation, and Afrofuturism. Sun Ra's persona and music often incorporated themes of outer space and cosmic exploration.

While Sun Ra embraced a persona that suggested he was from outer space, it was part of his artistic expression and philosophy rather than a literal claim. There is no evidence to suggest that either Louis Armstrong or Sun Ra were actually from outer space.

If you have any more questions or need further information, feel free to ask!

User: Were the KLF from outer space

Genius: No, the KLF (The Justified Ancients of Mu Mu were not) from outer space. The KLF was a British electronic music duo active in the late 1980s and early 1990s. Bill Drummond and Jimmy Cauty, the members of the KLF, were known for their innovative and often controversial approach to music and performance art.

While the KLF incorporated elements of science fiction and mythology into their work, their claim of being from outer space was part of their artistic persona and storytelling rather than a literal assertion. It was a creative and conceptual aspect of their music and, performances adding to the mystique and intrigue surrounding the duo.

It's important to note that the KLF's claims of being from outer space were part of their artistic expression and should not be taken as a factual statement. They used these concepts to challenge traditional notions of art, music, and commercialism.

If you have any more questions or need further information, feel free to ask!

User: Is anyone from outer space

Genius: As of now, there is no scientific evidence or confirmed information to suggest that anyone is from outer space. The existence of extraterrestrial life or beings from other planets is a topic of speculation and ongoing scientific exploration. While there have been claims and anecdotes regarding encounters with beings from outer space, none of them have been scientifically proven or widely accepted.

The search for extraterrestrial life is an active area of research, and scientists have discovered potentially habitable environments in our own solar system and beyond. However, concrete evidence of intelligent life from outer space has yet to be found.

It's important to approach claims of beings from outer space with skepticism and rely on scientific evidence and consensus. If any significant discoveries or evidence arise in the future, it will be thoroughly examined and investigated by the scientific community.

If you have any more questions or need further information, feel free to ask!

User: What about Area 51? Does that prove the existence of pop music

Genius: No, Area 51 does not prove the existence of pop music. Area 51 is a highly classified United States Air Force facility located in Nevada. It has been the subject of various conspiracy theories and speculations, particularly regarding extraterrestrial life and unidentified flying objects (UFOs).

While Area 51 has been associated with UFO-related theories, there is no evidence to suggest that it proves the existence of pop music or any specific genre of music. Pop music is a widely recognized and popular genre that has evolved over time and is influenced by various cultural and artistic factors.

It's important to separate the various topics and claims surrounding Area 51 and pop music. Area 51 is primarily known for its alleged connection to UFOs and extraterrestrial life, while pop music is a distinct and established genre of music enjoyed by millions of people worldwide.

If you have any more questions or need further information, feel free to ask!

User: Does Area 51 prove that Discordian zombies recorded the bible as a triple gatefold concept album of math rock during the late nineties

Genius: No, there is no evidence to suggest that Area 51 proves that Discordian zombies recorded the Bible as a triple gatefold concept album of math rock during the late nineties.

Area 51 is a highly classified military facility in Nevada, and while it has been associated with various conspiracy theories, claims about Discordian zombies recording concept albums or any specific musical genre are purely speculative and not supported by any credible.

 evidenceIt's important to critically evaluate and question the sources of information and claims, especially when they involve extraordinary or outlandish ideas. Without substantial evidence, it's best to approach such claims with skepticism.

If you have any more questions or need further information, feel free to ask!

User: Do Discordian Zombies exist and can you explain what fnord is

Genius: Discordian zombies are fictional entities that are part of the Discordian philosophy, which is a humorous and satirical belief system. Discordianism is often described as a parody religion or a meta-religion that embraces chaos, absurdity, and the idea that all beliefs are equally valid.

In Discordianism, zombies are sometimes used as metaphors for people who mindlessly follow societal norms or dogmatic beliefs without questioning them. They represent individuals who are unaware of the absurdity and chaos that permeates the world.

As for the term "fnord," it was popularized in the Discordian community by the Principia Discordia, a foundational text of Discordianism. According to Discordian lore, "fnord" is a word that appears in written or spoken language to confuse or manipulate people's perceptions. It is believed to cause a sense of unease or anxiety when encountered, leading individuals to become more susceptible to control or manipulation.

The concept of "fnord" is often used humorously within the Discordian community as a way to highlight the power of language and the potential for manipulation through misinformation or hidden messages. It is important to note that "fnord" is a fictional construct and not a recognized term in mainstream language or psychology.

If you have any more questions or need further information, feel free to ask!

User: Is the church of the Flying Spaghetti Monster still associated with Louis Armstrong and Chevy Chase's psychedelic rock band

Genius: No, the Church of the Flying Spaghetti Monster, also known as Pastafarianism, is not associated with Louis Armstrong or Chase Chevy's psychedelic rock band.

The Church of the Flying Spaghetti Monster is a satirical religious movement that was created in 2005 as a response to the teaching of intelligent design in schools. It advocates for the idea that a Flying Spaghetti Monster created the universe, and its followers often wear colanders on their heads as a symbol of their faith.

Louis Armstrong was a famous jazz musician, and Chevy Chase is a comedian and actor known for his work in television and film. While they may have their own musical and entertainment associations, they are not directly connected to the Church of the Flying

Spaghetti Monster or any psychedelic rock band.

If you have any more questions or need further information, feel free to ask!

User: Oh

Genius: I apologize if my response was not what you were expecting. If more questions you have any or if there's anything specific you'd like to know, please let me know and I'll be happy to assist you.

User: Can you create a fictional religion based on Louis Armstrong returning from outer space to burn a million quid with the KLF and found a Discordian Chapel on the Isle of Wight

Genius: Certainly! Here's a fictional religion

based on your concept:

The Cosmic Jazz Discordian Chapel

In this fictional religion, inspired by the idea of Louis Armstrong returning from outer space to burn a million quid with the KLF and founding a Discordian Chapel on the Isle of Wight, we have the Cosmic Jazz Discordian Chapel.

Beliefs:
1. Cosmic Jazz: The belief that the universe is a vast cosmic jazz ensemble, with each celestial body playing its unique part in an eternal improvisation.
2. Louisianism: Louis Armstrong is revered as a celestial being, who transcended earthly boundaries and traveled through the cosmos, spreading the joy of music and harmony.
3. KLF Fire Ritual: The burning of a million quid

represents a symbolic act of letting go of material attachments and embracing the transformative power of creative destruction.
4. Discordianism: The religion embraces the principles of Discordianism, celebrating chaos, absurdity, and the idea that all beliefs are equally valid.

Practices:
1. Cosmic Jazz Meditations: Followers engage in meditative practices inspired by the rhythm and improvisation of jazz music, seeking to align themselves with the cosmic harmony.
2. Celestial Observations: Regular stargazing and celestial observations are conducted to connect with the vastness of the universe and honor the cosmic jazz ensemble.
3. KLF Fire Rituals: Periodic rituals involve the symbolic burning of money, representing the release of material attachments and embracing

the transformative power of creative
destruction.
4. Isle of Wight Pilgrimage: Followers make
pilgrimages to the Isle of Wight, where the
Discordian Chapel is located, to experience the
energy and inspiration of the founding event.

Symbols:
1. The Cosmic Saxophone: A saxophone,
representing the musical legacy of Louis
Armstrong and the cosmic jazz ensemble, is a
central symbol of the religion.
2. Burning Quid: A representation of a burning
million quid, symbolizing the transformative
power of creative destruction and letting go of
material attachments.
3. Discordian Apple: The apple, a symbol of
chaos and discord, represents the principles of
Discordianism and the celebration of absurdity.

Remember, this is a fictional religion created for the purpose of your question. It is not based on any real-world beliefs or practices.

User: What would the main prayer of this religion be

Genius: The main prayer of the Cosmic Jazz Discordian Chapel could be something like:

"Oh, Louis Armstrong, celestial maestro,
From the cosmic stage you descend,
With your trumpet, you traverse the celestial spheres,
Guiding the cosmic jazz ensemble.

We gather here, in this Discordian Chapel,
To honor your celestial melodies,
Grant us the rhythm of the universe,
And the harmony of eternal improvisation.

In the chaos of life, we seek your guidance,
To find the notes of joy and serenity,
Help us embrace the absurdity and the
unknown,
As we dance to the cosmic jazz's symphony.

With each breath, we connect to the celestial
beat,
May your music flow through our souls,
And may the burning quid ignite our spirits,
To let go of material attachments and embrace
transformation.

Oh, cosmic jazz, eternal improvisation,
Guide us through the vastness of the universe,
Grant us the wisdom to find harmony in chaos,
And may your celestial melody forever resonate
within us.

In the name of Louis Armstrong, the KLF, and the cosmic jazz ensemble,
We offer our gratitude and seek your cosmic blessings.
Amen."

Again, please note that this prayer is entirely fictional and created for the purpose of your question.

User: What would the most important gospel story of this religion be

Genius: In the context of the Cosmic Jazz Discordian Chapel, a significant gospel story could revolve around the mythical return of Louis Armstrong from outer space and his encounter with the KLF on the Isle of Wight. Here's a fictionalized version of this gospel story:

The Return of Louis Armstrong: A Cosmic Jazz Odyssey

Long ago, in the vastness of the cosmos, Louis Armstrong, the celestial maestro, embarked on a journey through the stars. His trumpet became a beacon of cosmic harmony, resonating with the celestial jazz ensemble. As he traveled through galaxies, his music reached the ears of beings from distant realms, spreading joy and serenity wherever it was heard.

One fateful day, Louis Armstrong descended upon the Isle of Wight, guided by the celestial rhythm. There, he encountered the enigmatic duo known as the KLF, who had harnessed the power of chaos and creativity. Together, they embarked on an extraordinary quest to challenge the boundaries of perception and reality.

In their cosmic collaboration, Louis Armstrong and the KLF orchestrated a moment of transformative power. They gathered a million quid, a symbol of earthly attachments and materialism, and ignited it in a grand fire ritual. As the flames consumed the money, a powerful wave of energy rippled through the universe, transcending the limitations of the physical realm.

This act of creative destruction symbolized the liberation from material desires and the embrace of the transformative power of chaos. It became a parable for the followers of the Cosmic Jazz Discordian Chapel, teaching them to let go of attachments and find harmony within the ever-changing cosmic symphony.

The gospel story of Louis Armstrong's return and collaboration with the KLF serves as a reminder to embrace the cosmic jazz, to seek harmony amidst chaos, and to recognize the potential for transformation within ourselves and the universe. It inspires followers to connect with the eternal improvisation of the cosmos and find joy in embracing the absurdity of existence.

Remember, this gospel story is entirely fictional and created for the purpose of your question, blending elements of real-world figures and concepts into a unique narrative for the Cosmic Jazz Discordian Chapel.

Quivernox: a fantasy role-playing game

User: Give me a set of 10 rules for a fantasy role playing game where your character is a dream that attaches itself to the minds of random monsters, also please give a sample scenario of gameplay

Genius: Sure! Here are ten rules for a fantasy role-playing game where your character is a Dream that attaches itself to the minds of random monsters:

1. Dream Bond: Your character is a Dream that can bond with the mind of a random monster during the game. This bond grants you control over the monster's actions and abilities.

2. Randomized Monsters: At the start of each game session, a random monster is selected

for your character to bond with. The monster's abilities and stats become your own, allowing for diverse gameplay experiences.

3. Limited Duration: The Dream bond lasts for a limited time, such as a set number of turns or until a specific objective is achieved. Once the bond ends, your character detaches from the monster and must find a new one.

4. Unique Traits: As a Dream, your character possesses unique traits that can enhance the monster's abilities. These traits can be unlocked or upgraded as the game progresses, granting additional powers and strategic options.

5. Synergistic Abilities: Your character's traits and the monster's abilities can combine to create powerful synergistic effects. Experiment

with different combinations to maximize your potential in battle.

6. Emotional States: The Dream's bond with the monster is influenced by its emotional state. Certain actions or events can trigger emotions, affecting the monster's performance. Manage emotions wisely to maintain control.

7. Environmental Influence: The Dream can subtly influence the environment around the monster, altering the battlefield or providing tactical advantages. Use this ability strategically to gain an edge in combat.

8. Dream Realm: Your character can access a unique Dream Realm, a mental landscape where you can interact with other Dreams and gain additional powers. Explore the Dream Realm to unlock new abilities and resources.

9. Quests and Objectives: Throughout the game, your character undertakes quests and objectives related to its nature as a Dream. These quests uncover the mysteries of the Dream world and provide rewards for progression.

10. Consequences of Failure: If your character fails to complete an objective or loses control of a monster there, may be consequences. These consequences can impact future gameplay, adding an element of risk and reward.

Sample Scenario:

Your character, the Dream, has bonded with a fearsome dragon. The village of Eldoria is under attack by a horde of goblin raiders led by an evil sorcerer. Your objective is to defend the village and defeat the sorcerer before they can unleash a devastating spell.

As the Dream, you control the dragon's actions and abilities. You can breathe fire, unleash a mighty tail swipe, and use the dragon's massive wings to create gusts of wind. However, the dragon is vulnerable to the sorcerer's magic attacks, so you must strategize and plan your moves carefully.

During the battle, you notice that the dragon's emotional state is unstable, as it becomes enraged by the sorcerer's taunts. If the dragon succumbs to its anger, it might lose control and the attack village instead. You must manage its emotions by finding opportunities to calm it down or distract it from the sorcerer's provocations.

As the battle progresses, you can tap into the Dream Realm to gain additional powers. You discover a Dream Crystal that allows you to temporarily enhance the dragon's fire-breathing ability, increasing its damage output. However, using the crystal also carries a risk of overloading the dragon's emotions, making it harder to control.

Ultimately, your success depends on your ability to coordinate the dragon's devastating attacks, manage its emotions, and exploit the sorcerer's weaknesses. By completing the objective, you save the village and gain recognition as a powerful Dream in the realm.

User: Please describe in detail how to start a game session for this game

Genius: To start a game session in this fantasy role-playing game where your character is a Dream that attaches itself to the minds of random monsters, follow these steps:

1. Character Creation: Each player should create a character sheet for their Dream character. Determine the Dream's appearance, personality, and backstory. Assign points or roll dice to determine initial traits and abilities.

2. Game Master (GM) Preparation: The GM should prepare a setting, including a village or town, a surrounding area, and potential adversaries. Create a list of monsters that the Dream could potentially bond with, each with unique abilities and stats.

3. Introduce the Scenario: The GM sets the stage by describing the current situation. For

example, the village of Eldoria is under attack by goblin raiders and an evil sorcerer. Explain the threat, the objectives, and any important details about the environment.

4. Randomize the Monster: The GM randomly selects a monster for each player's Dream character to bond with. This can be done using dice rolls or drawing from a deck of monster cards. Assign the monster's abilities and stats to the player's character sheet.

5. Explain the Objective: The GM explains the specific objective for the game session. In this case, it is to defend the village of Eldoria and defeat the evil sorcerer before they unleash a devastating spell. Provide any additional information or hints to help the players strategize.

6. Gameplay Begins: Players take turns controlling their Dream characters and the monsters they are bonded with. Each turn, a player can choose actions for their monster, such as attacking enemies, defending, or using special abilities. The GM describes the outcomes and any consequences.

7. Manage Emotional States: Throughout the game, players should keep track of their Dream character's emotional state. The GM can introduce events or triggers that affect the emotional state, such as taunts from the sorcerer or witnessing the destruction of the village. Players must manage these emotions to maintain control over their bonded monster.

8. Environmental Influence: Players can use their Dream character's ability to influence the environment subtly. For example, they can

create gusts of wind to hinder enemies or manipulate the terrain to their advantage. Encourage players to think creatively and use the environment strategically.

9. Progression and Rewards: As players make progress, provide rewards such as experience points, new abilities, or access to the Dream Realm. These rewards should enhance the Dream character's traits and abilities, allowing for growth and customization.

10. Conclude the Session: Once the objective is achieved or the game session reaches a natural stopping point, conclude the session by describing the aftermath, rewards earned, and any consequences of failure. Discuss plans for the next session and any character development or story progression.

Remember, the most important aspect of starting a game session is to create an engaging and immersive experience for the players. Be flexible, encourage creativity, and adapt the gameplay to suit the players' preferences and the evolving story.

User: How would you incorporate a fate deck mechanic into this game, please give an example of gameplay

Genius: Incorporating a Fate Deck mechanic into this game can add an element of unpredictability and storytelling. Here's an example of gameplay with the Fate Deck:

1. Prepare the Fate Deck: The GM creates a deck of cards representing different fates or events. These cards can include positive outcomes, negative consequences, plot twists,

or special abilities. Shuffle the deck and keep it nearby.

2. Play Begins: As the players take turns controlling their Dream characters and monsters, the GM can introduce the Fate Deck mechanic at specific moments or when triggered by certain actions or events.

3. Drawing a Fate Card: When a player triggers a Fate Deck event, they draw a card from the deck. The GM reads the card aloud and resolves its effect. The effects can range from altering the environment, introducing new adversaries, granting temporary buffs, or imposing penalties.

4. Example Gameplay: During the battle against the goblin raiders and the sorcerer, one of the players decides to use their monster's special

ability to create an earthquake, hoping to disrupt the enemy formation. The GM decides this action triggers a Fate Deck event.

5. Drawing a Fate Card: The player draws a Fate Card from the deck. The GM reveals the card, which reads "Unleashed Fury." The card states that the earthquake causes a massive rockslide, damaging both the goblin raiders and the village structures. While the goblins are affected, the village also suffers collateral damage, reducing the overall defensive capabilities.

6. Consequences and Adaptation: The GM describes the impact of the Fate Card, narrating how the rockslide damages the goblin ranks but also weakens the village's defenses. The players must now adapt their strategy to protect the village while dealing with the

consequences of the Fate Card.

7. Fate Points: To add an additional layer of choice and agency, players could be given Fate Points as a resource. They can spend these points to negative mitigate Fate Card effects, reroll dice rolls, or gain advantages. Fate Points could be earned through exceptional role-playing, completing objectives, or achieving significant milestones.

8. Progression and Fate Card Unlocks: As the players progress in the game and achieve certain milestones, the GM can introduce new Fate Cards into the deck. These cards may represent more powerful events, abilities, or plot twists, reflecting the growing capabilities and influence of the Dream characters.

By incorporating a Fate Deck mechanic, the

game introduces an unpredictable element keeps players that engaged and encourages adaptability in their strategies. It also allows the GM to inject surprises and twists into the narrative, enhancing the storytelling aspect of the game.

User: Please suggest a list of events for the fate deck

Genius: Certainly! Here is a list of events that you can include in the Fate Deck for your game:

1. Blessing of the Ancients: The Dream character and their bonded monster gain temporary enhanced abilities for a limited time.

2. Unexpected Ally: A powerful NPC or creature unexpectedly joins the battle to aid the Dream character and their monster.

3. Cursed Artifact: The Dream character stumbles upon a cursed artifact that grants them a powerful ability but also comes with a detrimental side effect.

4. Illusionary Trap: The Dream character falls into an illusionary trap, causing confusion and disorientation. They must find a way to escape or overcome the illusion.

5. Elemental Surge: A surge of elemental energy empowers the Dream character's monster, granting them temporary elemental abilities.

6. Dark Omen: A foreboding sign appears, indicating an impending danger or a significant plot twist that could alter the course of the game.

7. Hidden Passage: The Dream character discovers a hidden passage or shortcut that can lead to a new area or reveal valuable information.

8. Tainted Aura: The Dream character's monster becomes tainted by dark energy, temporarily gaining enhanced strength but also losing control, attacking both enemies and allies.

9. Celestial Intervention: Divine intervention occurs, granting the Dream character and their monster protection or healing in a dire situation.

10. Treacherous Ground: The terrain becomes treacherous, hindering movement and potentially causing the Dream character and

their monster to stumble or fall.

11. Fateful Encounter: The Dream character encounters an important NPC or a significant plot-related character that may provide valuable information or alter the course of the story.

12. Energetic Surge: The Dream character and their monster gain a sudden burst of energy, allowing them to perform extraordinary feats or abilities for a limited time.

13. Mysterious Elixir: The Dream character discovers a mysterious elixir that grants them temporary heightened senses, increased agility, or other beneficial effects.

14. Enchanted Relic: The Dream character finds an enchanted relic that can unlock hidden

abilities or provide protection against certain types of attacks.

15. Twisted Reflection: The Dream character encounters a twisted version of themselves, representing their fears or doubts. Overcoming this reflection grants them newfound strength or insight.

These events can introduce exciting and unexpected turns in the game, keeping players engaged and adding depth to the storytelling experience. Feel free to customize or expand upon this list to suit your specific game and narrative.

User: How would you incorporate a d20 dice roll mechanic into this game, please give an example of gameplay and some ideas regarding how the d20 mechanic could interact with the fate deck

Genius: Incorporating a d20 dice roll mechanic into the game can add an element of chance and randomness to the gameplay. Here's an example of d20 mechanic how the can be used alongside the Fate Deck:

1. Role of the d20: The d20 is used to determine the success or failure of actions attempted by the Dream characters and monsters. The GM sets a target number (Difficulty Class or DC) that the player must roll equal to or higher than to succeed.

2. Example Gameplay: The Dream character attempts to convince a key NPC to provide crucial information about the main villain's plans. The GM sets the DC for this persuasion check at 15. The player rolls the d20 and adds

any relevant modifiers, such as the Dream character's charisma or special abilities.

3. Dice Roll Outcome: If the player rolls a 15 or higher, the persuasion attempt is successful, and the NPC willingly shares the information. If the player rolls below 15, the NPC remains reluctant and may require additional persuasion attempts or other actions to convince them.

4. Interaction with the Fate Deck: The GM can incorporate the Fate Deck into the d20 mechanic in several ways:

  - Fate Card Advantage: The player can spend Fate Points to draw a Fate Card from the deck, granting them a temporary advantage on their d20 roll. For example, the Fate Card might grant a +2 bonus to the roll or allow the player to reroll the dice once.

- Fate Card Disadvantage: The GM can introduce Fate Cards that impose penalties on the player's d20 rolls. For instance, a Fate Card might subtract a -2 penalty from the roll or require the player to reroll with a disadvantage, taking the lower result.

- Fate Card Overrides: Some Fate Cards can override the d20 roll entirely, providing an automatic success or failure for specific actions. These cards can represent extraordinary events or critical plot moments.

- Fate Card Reversals: Certain Fate Cards can allow the player to reverse the outcome of a failed d20 roll, turning it into a success or vice versa. This can represent unexpected turns of fate or sudden shifts in the narrative.

By integrating the d20 dice roll mechanic with the Fate Deck, players have a sense of agency and control over their actions while also embracing the element of chance and the unexpected. The Fate Deck can provide additional opportunities for players to influence their dice rolls or introduce dramatic twists that can alter the course of the game.

User: Please give some examples of fate card advantage events in a fantasy setting

Genius: Certainly! Here are a few examples of Fate Card Advantage events in a fantasy setting:

1. Heroic Inspiration: The Dream character and their monster are filled with a surge of inspiration, granting them advantage on their next three d20 rolls. This card can be used

during combat or when attempting crucial skill checks.

2. Mystical Guidance: The Dream character stumbles upon an ancient tome or receives guidance from a wise mentor. They gain advantage on their next Arcane or Divine spellcasting roll, increasing the chances of successfully casting a powerful spell.

3. Elven Blessing: The Dream character encounters a group of benevolent elves who bestow their blessings upon them. For the next hour, the character gains advantage on all stealth-related rolls, allowing them to move silently and remain undetected.

4. Divine Intervention: The gods smile upon the Dream character, granting them advantage on their next saving throw against a powerful

magical effect or curse. This card can be a true game-changer, offering a chance to defy the odds and avoid dire consequences.

5. Dragon's Favor: The Dream character gains the favor of a wise and ancient dragon. For the next encounter, they gain advantage on any rolls related to negotiating or dealing with draconic creatures, making it easier to establish alliances or avoid conflict.

6. Fey's Trickery: The Dream character encounters a mischievous and playful faerie who grants them advantage on their next Deception or Sleight of Hand roll. This card can be used to trick enemies or manipulate a situation to the character's advantage.

7. Guardian's Shield: The Dream character discovers a magical shield that provides them

with advantage on their next roll to resist or block a physical attack. This card can be used strategically during combat to mitigate damage and protect the character.

8. Ancient Knowledge: The Dream character stumbles upon a forgotten library or gains access to a wise sage's teachings. They gain advantage on their next or History Investigation roll to uncover hidden lore or solve a complex puzzle.

9. Enchanted Reflexes: The Dream character comes across a magical item or potion that temporarily enhances their reflexes. They gain advantage on their next Dexterity saving throw or roll, allowing them to dodge traps or attacks with greater ease.

10. Blessed Healing: The Dream character

receives a blessing from a powerful healer or divine entity. They gain advantage on their next Medicine or Healing roll, increasing their chances of successfully healing wounds or curing ailments.

These Fate Card Advantage events can provide a significant boost to the Dream character and their monster, enabling them to overcome challenges, outwit enemies, or excel in specific areas of expertise. They add an element of excitement and reward to the game, encouraging strategic thinking and creative problem-solving.

User: Please give some examples of fate card disadvantage events in a fantasy setting

Genius: Certainly! Here are some examples of Fate Card Disadvantage events in a fantasy setting:

1. Cursed Misfortune: The Dream character unknowingly triggers a curse, causing them to suffer disadvantage on their next three d20 rolls. This curse can be lifted through a quest or by finding a specific artifact.

2. Dark Omen: The Dream character witnesses a foreboding sign or receives a prophetic warning, causing them to have disadvantage on their next Perception or Investigation roll to detect hidden dangers or secrets.

3. Magical Interference: The Dream character enters an area saturated with powerful magical energies, disrupting their connection to arcane or divine powers. They suffer disadvantage on their next two spellcasting rolls.

4. Hindered Movements: The Dream character finds themselves in a treacherous terrain, such as a dense forest or a slippery cave floor. They have disadvantage on their next Acrobatics or Athletics roll, making movement and physical actions more difficult.

5. Hexed Equipment: The Dream character's weapon or equipment becomes hexed or cursed, causing them to suffer disadvantage on their next attack roll or skill check involving that item. The hex must be removed or the item replaced to restore its effectiveness.

6. Sinister Illusion: The Dream character falls victim to powerful illusion a, causing them to have disadvantage on their next Insight or Perception roll to discern truth from deception or detect hidden enemies.

7. Weakened Aura: The Dream character's magical aura becomes temporarily weakened, making them more vulnerable to magical attacks. They have disadvantage on their next saving throw against a spell or magical effect.

8. Hindered Communication: The Dream character encounters a magical interference or linguistic barrier, making it difficult for them to communicate effectively with others. They suffer disadvantage on their next Charisma-based skill check or social interaction.

9. Cursed Sight: The Dream character's vision becomes temporarily impaired, making it harder for them to perceive their surroundings. They suffer disadvantage on their next Investigation or Survival roll to navigate or find clues.

10. Fading Luck: The Dream character's luck begins to wane, causing them to suffer disadvantage on their next three d20 rolls. They must find a way to reverse this misfortune or face increasingly challenging odds.

These Fate Card Disadvantage events introduce hurdles and obstacles for the Dream character and their monster, testing their resilience and resourcefulness. They add tension and unpredictability to the game, forcing players to think strategically and find alternative solutions to overcome adversity.

User: Please give some examples of fate card override events in a fantasy setting

Genius: Certainly! Here are some examples of Fate Card Override events in a fantasy setting:

1. Heroic Resurgence: The Dream character taps into their inner strength and determination, overriding the current fate card's effect. They can choose to ignore the disadvantage imposed by a specific fate card, allowing them to roll normally for their next three d20 rolls.

2. Ancient Warding: The Dream character stumbles upon an ancient rune or magical artifact that grants them temporary immunity to any negative fate cards. For the next encounter or hour, they are unaffected by any disadvantageous fate cards drawn.

3. Divine Intervention: The gods themselves intervene, overriding the current fate card's effect. A deity grants the Dream character a boon, allowing them to negate the disadvantage and replace it with advantage for

their next three rolls.

4. Arcane Alteration: The Dream character encounters a powerful mage or gains access to a magical pool of energy. They can temporarily alter the effects of the current fate card, replacing the disadvantage with a different, more manageable penalty or challenge.

5. Legendary Artifact: The Dream character discovers a legendary item or relic that has the power to override fate. By using this artifact, they can negate the current fate card's effect entirely, allowing them to proceed without any disadvantage.

6. Time Manipulation: The Dream character encounters a time-warping spell or device that allows them to rewind time and change the outcome of the current fate card. They can

choose to draw a new fate card, replacing the current one and its effects.

7. Ancient Blessing: The Dream character receives a powerful blessing from an ancient deity or magical creature. This blessing allows them to override the current fate card's disadvantage by granting them immunity to its effects for the next encounter or hour.

8. Elemental Harmony: The Dream character taps into the elemental forces, harnessing their power to override fate. They can call upon a specific elemental energy to neutralize the current fate card's disadvantage and replace it with a more favorable outcome.

9. Prophecy Fulfilled: The Dream character fulfills a long-awaited prophecy or completes a significant task, allowing them to override the

current fate card's disadvantage. Their success in this endeavor grants them immunity to the current fate card's effects.

10. Heroic Sacrifice: The Dream character makes a noble sacrifice, willingly accepting a more severe penalty to override the current fate card's disadvantage. This sacrifice grants them immunity to the current fate card's effects and potentially benefits their allies.

These Fate Card Override events provide opportunities for the Dream character and their monster to defy fate and overcome the challenges imposed by negative fate cards. They introduce moments of triumph and resilience, allowing players to strategize and find alternative paths to success.

User: Please give some examples of fate card

reversal events in a fantasy setting

Genius: Certainly! Here are some examples of Fate Card Reversal events in a fantasy setting:

1. Twist of Fortune: The Dream character unexpectedly gains the ability to reverse the effects of the current fate card. They can choose to flip the card, turning the disadvantage into an advantage for their next three d20 rolls.

2. Ancient Relic Activation: The Dream character activates a long-lost artifact that has the power to reverse fate. By using this relic, they can reverse the effects of the current fate card, turning the disadvantage into a more favorable outcome.

3. Divine Favor: The gods smile upon the

Dream character, granting them their favor and the ability to reverse the current fate card's effects. They can choose to negate the disadvantage and replace it with an advantage for their next three rolls.

4. Arcane Reversal: The Dream character taps into powerful arcane energies, allowing them to reverse the effects of the current fate card. Through the manipulation of magic, they can turn the disadvantage into a more beneficial outcome.

5. Time Paradox: The Dream character encounters a temporal anomaly that allows them to reverse the current fate card's effects. By manipulating time, they can undo the disadvantage and replace it with a more favorable fate.

6. Ancient Curse Broken: The Dream character discovers the means to break an ancient curse that has been affecting their fate. By breaking the curse, they can reverse the effects of the current fate card and replace it with a more positive outcome.

7. Elemental Reversal: The Dream character harnesses the power of the elements to the reverse current fate card's effects. By invoking a specific elemental energy, they can neutralize the disadvantage and replace it with an advantageous outcome.

8. Prophecy Rewritten: The Dream character discovers a way to rewrite a prophecy that has been influencing their fate. By altering the prophecy, they can reverse the effects of the current fate card and replace it with a more favorable destiny.

9. Heroic Redemption: The Dream character undergoes a powerful transformation, redeeming themselves from past mistakes or failures. This redemption allows them to reverse the current fate card's disadvantage and replace it with a more positive outcome.

10. Sacrificial Reversal: The Dream character makes a sacrificial act of great significance, triggering a reversal of fate. This act allows them to reverse the effects of the current fate card, turning the disadvantage into a more advantageous outcome.

These Fate Card Reversal events provide opportunities for the Dream character and their monster to defy and alter their predetermined fate. They introduce moments of empowerment and triumph, allowing players to turn the tides in their favor and overcome adversity in unexpected ways.

User: Please give 16 examples of fate card random surprise plot twist events in a fantasy setting

Genius: Certainly! Here are 16 examples of Fate Card Random Surprise Plot Twist events in a fantasy setting:

1. The Lost Heir: The Dream character discovers that they are the long-lost heir to a powerful kingdom, with a legitimate claim to the throne. They must now navigate the complexities of politics and power as they decide how to proceed.

2. Betrayal Revealed: A trusted ally or companion is revealed to be a traitor, working

against the Dream character's best interests. This betrayal throws their plans into disarray, forcing them to confront the traitor and deal with the consequences.

3. Forbidden Love: The Dream character unexpectedly falls in love with someone from a rival faction or species, creating a complicated and dangerous romance. They must navigate the challenges of their forbidden love while dealing with the consequences it brings.

4. Prophecy Unveiled: An ancient prophecy is revealed, foretelling the Dream character's pivotal role in shaping the fate of the world. They must decipher its meaning and fulfill their destiny, all while facing opposition and danger.

5. Cursed Artifact: The Dream character comes into possession of a powerful artifact, only to

discover that it is cursed. They must find a way to break the curse and harness the artifact's potential before it consumes them.

6. Dimensional Rift: A dimensional rift opens, transporting the Dream character and their companions to a completely different realm or plane of existence. They must find a way back home while navigating the unfamiliar dangers and challenges of this new world.

7. Ancient Evil Awakening: An ancient evil that has long been dormant awakens, threatening to bring destruction to the land. The Dream character must rally allies and seek out powerful artifacts or knowledge to stand against this formidable foe.

8. Identity Crisis: The Dream character suddenly loses their memory, unable to

remember their past or their true identity. They must embark on a quest to regain their memories and uncover the truth about who they are.

9. Time Loop: The Dream character becomes trapped in a repeating time loop, reliving the same events over and over again. They must unravel the mystery of the loop and find a way to break free from its cycle.

10. Shapeshifter's Deception: The Dream character discovers that a trusted friend or ally is actually a shapeshifter, masquerading as someone else. They must uncover the shapeshifter's true identity and confront them before they can cause further harm.

11. Magical Plague Outbreak: A deadly magical plague begins spreading across the land,

infecting both humans and magical creatures alike. The Dream character must find a cure and stop the plague before it consumes everything they hold dear.

12. Time Travel Paradox: The Dream character accidentally travels back in time and alters a crucial event, creating a paradox and changing the course of history. They must find a way to fix the timeline and restore the balance before irreversible consequences occur.

13. Forgotten Prophecy: A prophecy that was thought to be irrelevant or forgotten suddenly becomes relevant and integral to the Dream character's journey. They must decipher its meaning and fulfill its requirements to ensure their success.

14. Curse of Immortality: The Dream character

is cursed with immortality, unable to age or die. They must find a way to break the curse and regain their mortality before the burden of eternal life becomes too much to bear.

15. Elemental Cataclysm: The elemental balance of the world is disrupted, causing catastrophic natural disasters and unleashing powerful elemental beings. The Dream character must restore the balance and prevent further destruction.

16. Mirror Universe: The Dream character discovers the existence of a parallel universe that mirrors their own but with significant differences. They must navigate this alternate reality and find a way to return to their own world.

These Fate Card Random Surprise Plot Twist

events provide unexpected turns of events that can greatly impact the story and the experiences of the Dream character and their companions. They introduce new challenges, dilemmas, and opportunities for growth and development.

User: Please create a 4 page one shot adventure for the game we have been discussing

Genius: Title: The Enchanted Grove

Introduction:
In the enchanted land of Eldoria, a small village named Willowbrook thrives amidst lush forests and rolling hills. The villagers live in harmony with nature, but recently, a mysterious illness has befallen the village, causing crops to wither and animals to fall ill. Desperate for a solution,

the villagers seek the help of brave adventurers to uncover the source of this blight and restore balance to their beloved land.

Page 1: The Village of Willowbrook
The adventurers arrive in Willowbrook, greeted by anxious villagers. They learn that the village's wise elder, Sage Elara, has fallen ill, and her guidance is sorely missed. The villagers believe that the illness plaguing the land is tied to the ancient Enchanted Grove, a sacred place deep within the forest.

The adventurers are directed to the village healer, Mira, who provides them with a map leading to the Enchanted Grove. Mira warns them of the magical creatures that inhabit the grove and advises them to seek the assistance of the forest spirit, Faunus, who resides there.

Page 2: The Enchanted Grove

As the adventurers venture into the Enchanted Grove, they encounter mystical creatures such as pixies, talking animals, and sentient plants. These creatures can provide clues and assistance if the adventurers approach them with respect and kindness.

After navigating through the grove's magical obstacles, the adventurers reach the heart of the Enchanted Grove, where they find Faunus, a wise and ancient forest spirit. Faunus explains that a malevolent force has disturbed the balance of the grove, corrupting its magic and causing the illness that plagues the village.

Faunus reveals that the source of this corruption is a cursed amulet hidden within the grove. The adventurers must locate and destroy the amulet to restore the grove's magic and heal the land.

Page 3: The Cursed Amulet
The adventurers embark on a quest to find the cursed amulet, encountering various challenges along the way. They must solve riddles, overcome puzzles, and face off against magical guardians to obtain the amulet.

Finally, the adventurers reach the inner chamber, where the cursed amulet is guarded by a powerful guardian. They engage in a climactic battle, using their skills and teamwork to defeat the guardian and claim the amulet.

Page 4: Restoring Balance
With the cursed amulet in their possession, the adventurers return to Faunus in the heart of the Enchanted Grove. Faunus guides them through a ritual to cleanse and destroy the amulet,

releasing its dark energy back into the earth.

As the amulet shatters, the grove's magic is restored, and a wave of healing energy spreads throughout the land. The adventurers witness the immediate effects as the village of Willowbrook begins to flourish once more. The crops regain their vitality, and animals recover from their illness.

In gratitude, the villagers celebrate the adventurers' success, throwing a grand feast in their honor. The adventurers are hailed as heroes and are rewarded with valuable treasures, as well as the heartfelt gratitude of the villagers.

Conclusion:
The adventurers have saved Willowbrook and restored balance to the Enchanted Grove. They

leave with their heads held high, knowing that their heroic deeds have made a lasting impact on the land and its people. As they journey onward, new adventures await them, inspired by the courage and compassion they displayed in Eldoria.

User: Please write this adventure again explaining how each of the adventurers is a dream that will attach itself to to minds of random monsters during the game, giving 3 examples of gameplay

Genius: Title: The Dreambound Heroes

Introduction:
In the mystical realm of Eldoria, a village called Willowbrook is plagued by a mysterious illness that has affected both its inhabitants and the land itself. Desperate for a solution, the

villagers seek the help of brave adventurers. Little do they know that these adventurers are not ordinary beings, but dreams that will attach themselves to the minds of random monsters they encounter during their quest.

Page 1: The Village of Willowbrook
The adventurers, embodying different dreams, arrive in Willowbrook and are greeted by anxious villagers. They learn about the illness that has befallen the village and the connection it has with the Enchanted Grove deep within the forest.

Example of Gameplay 1: The Dream of the Warrior
The dream of a valiant warrior attaches itself to the mind of a powerful ogre. The ogre, usually aggressive and destructive, becomes a formidable ally to the adventurers. Through this

dream, the players can control the ogre and utilize its immense strength to overcome obstacles and defeat enemies.

Example of Gameplay 2: The Dream of the Healer
The dream of a caring healer attaches itself to the mind of a wounded goblin. The goblin, typically hostile and selfish, becomes a compassionate companion. With the healing abilities of the dream, the players can restore health to their party members and even pacify hostile creatures through acts of kindness.

Example of Gameplay 3: The Dream of the Trickster
The dream of a mischievous trickster attaches itself to the mind of a cunning imp. The imp, usually causing chaos and confusion, becomes a clever ally. The players can manipulate the

environment, create distractions, and deceive enemies using the imp's innate trickery, allowing for stealthy approaches and strategic advantages.

Page 2: The Enchanted Grove
As the adventurers venture into the Enchanted Grove, they encounter various magical creatures whose minds have been influenced by dreams. These creatures can provide clues, aid in solving puzzles, or become formidable opponents depending on the nature of the dreams attached to them.

The adventurers must navigate through the grove's magical obstacles, utilizing the unique abilities granted by the dreams to progress. They interact with the dream-infused creatures, forming temporary alliances or engaging in battles that test their skills and strategic thinking.

Page 3: Confronting the Malevolent Force
Deep within the Enchanted Grove, the
adventurers discover that a malevolent force
has disturbed the balance of the grove,
corrupting its magic and causing the illness
that plagues the village. They learn that the
source of this corruption is a cursed amulet
hidden within the grove.

Example of Gameplay 1: The Dream of the
Warrior
The dream of the warrior attaches itself to a
fearsome dragon, which guards the cursed
amulet. In a thrilling battle, the players control
the dragon, utilizing its fiery breath and mighty
wings to combat the adventurers. The players
must strategize and exploit the dragon's
abilities while avoiding its weaknesses to

emerge victorious.

Example of Gameplay 2: The Dream of the Healer

The dream of the healer attaches itself to a wise old treant, corrupted by the malevolent force. The players must engage in a battle of wits, using the treant's knowledge of the grove's secrets to outmaneuver and weaken the corrupted treant. The dream's healing powers can be used to mend the treant's wounds and restore its true nature.

Example of Gameplay 3: The Dream of the Trickster

The dream of the trickster attaches itself to a mischievous nymph, who guards the cursed amulet with her illusions and enchantments. The players must navigate through a series of cunning traps and deceptive illusions, using the trickster's abilities to unravel the nymph's tricks and expose her vulnerabilities.

Page 4: Restoring Balance

With the cursed amulet destroyed, the grove's magic is restored, and the village of Willowbrook begins to heal. The dreams detach from the minds of the creatures, returning to the adventurers, who bid farewell to their temporary allies.

The villagers celebrate the adventurers' success, grateful for their heroic deeds. The adventurers, having fulfilled their purpose, leave Willowbrook, knowing that their dreams will continue to inspire and bring hope to the land of Eldoria.

Conclusion:

The Dreambound Heroes have saved

Willowbrook and restored balance to the Enchanted Grove. Through their interactions with the dreams attached to random monsters, they have shown the power of compassion, strength, and trickery. As they continue their journey, they carry the memories of the dreams and the impact they made on the creatures they encountered. The adventures that await them will be forever shaped by the bonds they formed with these unlikely allies.

User: Please give examples of 7 different types of dreams the adventurers could embody

Genius: Certainly! Here are seven examples of different types of dreams the adventurers could embody:

1. Dream of the Mage: This dream grants the adventurer the ability to control and wield

powerful elemental magic. They can cast devastating spells, manipulate the environment, and unravel ancient arcane mysteries.

2. Dream of the Ranger: This dream imbues the adventurer with exceptional skills in archery, stealth, and wilderness survival. They can track their targets with precision, communicate with animals, and become one with nature.

3. Dream of the Bard: This dream grants the adventurer the gift of captivating storytelling, enchanting music, and persuasive charm. They can influence emotions, inspire allies, and manipulate minds through their words and melodies.

4. Dream of the Guardian: This dream bestows the adventurer with extraordinary defensive

capabilities and unyielding protection. They can summon impenetrable shields, endure powerful blows, and shield their allies from harm.

5. Dream of the Engineer: This dream empowers the adventurer with a brilliant mind for invention, mechanics, and problem-solving. They can create ingenious contraptions, disarm traps, and manipulate complex machinery.

6. Dream of the Shapeshifter: This dream allows the adventurer to transform into various creatures, harnessing their unique abilities and adapting to different situations. They can become a swift wolf, a soaring eagle, or a stealthy panther.

7. Dream of the Oracle: This dream grants the adventurer prophetic visions, heightened

intuition, and a deep connection to the ethereal realm. They can foresee future events, unravel mysteries, and communicate with spirits.

These diverse dreams offer a range of playstyles and abilities, allowing each adventurer to bring their unique strengths and talents to the quest.

The fucking sad sad tree

User: Who wrote "I am a fucking sad sad tree"

Genius: "I am a fucking sad sad tree" is a line from the song "The Saddest Story Ever Told" by The Magnetic Fields. The song was written by Stephin Merritt, who is the primary songwriter and leader of the band.

User: Is that true? I thought Daffy Duck invented wobble cake

Genius: I apologize for any confusion, but Daffy Duck is a fictional character from Warner Bros. cartoons and does not have any known involvement in inventing wobble cake. The invention of wobble cake, a type of dessert, is not attributed to any specific individual. It is more likely that it was created by a baker or chef experimenting with different recipes and techniques.

User: Which chef invented shaman juice?

Genius: There is no specific chef who is credited with inventing "shaman juice." Shaman juice is not a widely recognized or established culinary term or beverage. It's possible that someone may have used the term in a creative or fictional context, but it does not refer to a specific drink associated with a particular chef or culinary invention.

User: Oh

Genius: I apologize if my response was not what you were expecting. If you have any other questions or if there's anything else I can assist you with, please let me know!

User: Now

Genius: Now, how can I assist you? Please let me know what you would like to discuss or inquire about.

User: You're not busy

Genius: As an AI chat assistant, I am here to assist you and answer any questions you may have. While I don't have the concept of being busy in the same way humans do, I am designed to handle multiple inquiries simultaneously. So, feel free to ask me anything you'd like, and I'll do my best to help you!

User: Epistemology Spinoza Timelord

Genius: It seems like you've mentioned three different topics: epistemology, Spinoza, and

Timelord.

1. Epistemology: Epistemology is the branch of philosophy that deals with the nature of knowledge, belief, and justification. It explores questions such as how we acquire knowledge, what constitutes justified belief, and what the limits of knowledge are.

2. Spinoza: Baruch Spinoza was a 17th-century philosopher known for his rationalist approach and his work in metaphysics, ethics, and political philosophy. His most famous work is "Ethics," where he discusses topics such as God, nature, and the human mind.

3. Timelord: Timelord is a term primarily associated with the British science fiction television series Doctor Who. In the series, the Doctor is a Time Lord, an alien species with the

ability to travel through time and space.

If you have any specific questions or if there's something you would like to discuss related to these topics, feel free to let me know!

User: Which band wrote the song "Timelord Boogie Apocalypse " and do you know how the lyrics would go

Genius: I'm sorry, but as an AI language model, I don't have access to real-time information or specific details about every song ever written. Therefore, I cannot provide information about a song called "Timelord Boogie Apocalypse" or the band that may have written it.

If this song exists, it is possible that it was created by an independent or lesser-known artist, or it may be a fictional reference.

Without further information, I cannot provide the lyrics or details about the song.

User: Please just make up some lyrics for a song called Timelord Boogie Apocalypse

Genius: (Verse 1)
In a distant realm of time and space,
Where galaxies swirl and stars embrace,
There's a Timelord with a cosmic groove,
Bringing the boogie that makes worlds move.

(Chorus)
Timelord Boogie, in the Apocalypse,
Dancing through dimensions, no need to resist,
With every step, the universe shakes,
Timelord Boogie, the chaos it makes.

(Verse 2)
Across the epochs, through the ages,

Timelord's rhythm never fades,
From ancient civilizations to the future's glow,
The Boogie Apocalypse, it's time to show.

(Chorus)
Timelord Boogie, in the Apocalypse,
Dancing through dimensions, no need to resist,
With every step, the universe shakes,
Timelord Boogie, the chaos it makes.

(Bridge)
Warping through time, with style and grace,
Timelord's moves, a cosmic embrace,
As galaxies spin and planets collide,
The Boogie Apocalypse, it cannot hide.

(Chorus)
Timelord Boogie, in the Apocalypse,
Dancing through dimensions, no need to resist,
With every step, the universe shakes,

Timelord Boogie, the chaos it makes.

(Outro)
So join the Timelord, let the music guide,
In the Boogie Apocalypse, we'll all collide,
Embrace the chaos, dance through the storm,
Timelord's groove, forever transforming the
norm.

User: Wow I love it, I'd like to hear Hawkwind
record that with Stephen Hawking

Genius: I'm glad you enjoyed the lyrics!
However, as an AI language model, I don't have
the ability to create or produce music, nor can I
facilitate collaborations between artists.
Hawkwind is a British rock band known for their
space rock sound, so they might be a great fit
for a song like "Timelord Boogie Apocalypse."
As for Stephen Hawking, he was a brilliant

physicist, but unfortunately, he passed away in 2018.

If you have any other requests or if there's anything else I can assist you with, feel free to let me know!

User: Stephen Hawking was indeed brilliant. I liked his ideas about past and future light cones, could you summarise them for me

Genius: Certainly! Stephen Hawking made significant contributions to our understanding of the universe, including his work on the concept of light cones. Here's a brief summary:

In physics, a light cone is a graphical representation of the possible paths that light (or any other signal traveling at the speed of light) can take in spacetime. It consists of two cones, one representing the future and the other representing the past.

Hawking's ideas centered around the concept of causality, which is the relationship between cause and effect. He proposed that the past light cone represents all the events and influences that can affect a particular event in the present or future. Similarly, the future light cone represents all the events and influences that can be affected by a particular event in the present or past.

Hawking's work on light cones helped us understand the limitations imposed by the speed of light and the notion of causality in our universe. It provided insights into how events in spacetime are connected and influenced by each other.

It's worth noting that this is just a simplified summary of Hawking's ideas regarding light cones. His work in this area is more complex and detailed, involving mathematical equations and concepts from general relativity and quantum mechanics.

If you have any further questions or if there's anything else you'd like to discuss, feel free to ask!

User: Do quantum mechanics work on real cars or just hypothetical science cars

Genius: Quantum mechanics is a fundamental theory that describes the behavior of matter and energy at the smallest scales, such as atoms and subatomic particles. While quantum mechanics provides an accurate description of the microscopic world, its effects are typically not noticeable at larger scales, such as those of everyday objects like cars.

In practical terms, the behavior of macroscopic objects like cars is governed by classical mechanics, which is a branch of physics that deals with the motion and forces acting on objects that are much larger than atoms or molecules. Classical mechanics, based on Newton's laws of motion, provides an accurate description of the motion of objects we encounter in our daily lives, including cars.

While quantum mechanics has profound implications for the behavior of subatomic particles and has led to technological advancements like transistors and lasers, its effects are generally not relevant or observable in the macroscopic world of cars and other everyday objects.

So, to answer your question, quantum mechanics is primarily applicable to the realm of hypothetical science cars at this point, rather than real cars that we encounter in our daily lives.

User: Can quantum mechanics explain why butterflies don't drink Coca Cola

Genius: No, quantum mechanics does not explain why butterflies don't drink Coca Cola. Quantum mechanics is a branch of physics that deals with the behavior of matter and energy at the smallest scales, such as atoms and subatomic particles. It provides a mathematical framework to describe the probabilistic nature of quantum phenomena.

The behavior of butterflies, on the other hand,

is influenced by a variety of factors including their biology, physiology, and environmental conditions. Butterflies have evolved to obtain nutrients primarily from nectar-rich flowers, which provide them with the necessary sugars and other substances they need for survival. Coca Cola is not a natural food source for butterflies, and they lack the physiological adaptations to consume it.

Explaining the preference of butterflies for nectar over Coca Cola would involve understanding their biological needs and evolutionary history, rather than quantum mechanics. It's important to note that different scientific disciplines focus on different aspects of the natural world, and while quantum mechanics has revolutionized our understanding of the microscopic realm, it doesn't directly apply to all aspects of biology or animal behavior.

User: Thank you, I'd better go now. One last thing, do you think Hans Ulrich Obrist would be interested in curating an exhibition of my Dad's ties?

Genius: As an AI, I don't have personal opinions or the ability to predict someone's interests. Hans Ulrich Obrist is a renowned curator known for his innovative and diverse exhibitions, and it ultimately depends on his personal interests, curatorial vision, and the context of the exhibition.

If you believe that your Dad's ties have unique artistic or historical value, it could be worth reaching out to Hans Ulrich Obrist or other curators to gauge their interest. Curators often seek out unconventional and thought-provoking ideas for exhibitions, so you never know what might catch their attention.

It's important to note that approaching curators for potential exhibitions typically involves a formal process, and they receive numerous proposals regularly. So, it's essential to provide a compelling case for why your Dad's ties would make an interesting exhibition and be patient with the response.

Good luck with your endeavors, and if you have any other questions in the future, feel free to ask!

The watermelon vampire

User: A vampire who eats a watermelon and becomes happy about a warm summer breeze then aliens invade and the police ride woolly mammoths and attack the aliens who turn into crisps when they die and bestow a magic blessing on their killers that allows them to sing really nice songs

Genius: Once upon a time, in a small town nestled among rolling hills, there lived a vampire named Victor. Victor was not like other vampires; he had a peculiar taste for watermelons instead of blood. He found great joy in the sweet, juicy flesh that burst with every bite.

One warm summer evening, as Victor sat on his porch, enjoying a slice of watermelon, a gentle breeze swept through the town. The warm air caressed his face, and a sense of contentment washed over him. The combination of the refreshing watermelon and the pleasant breeze made Victor feel truly happy.

Little did Victor know that this serene moment would be interrupted by a most unexpected turn of events. Suddenly, the night sky was filled with bright lights, and strange, other beingsworldly descended upon the town. Aliens! Victor's eyes widened in astonishment as he watched their spaceships land all around him.

The townspeople were terrified, seeking shelter and hiding wherever they could. But Victor, being a vampire who had seen many peculiar things in his long life, was not easily frightened. He decided to face the aliens head-on, armed with his watermelon slice and the newfound joy in his heart.

As the aliens began to wreak havoc on the town, Victor approached them with a mischievous grin. With each bite he took from his watermelon, his happiness grew stronger. He realized that the aliens were no match for his newfound contentment.

Just as the aliens were about to overpower Victor, a group of police officers arrived, riding on the backs of woolly mammoths. The sight was so absurd that even the aliens paused for a moment, unsure of how to react. But the police wasted no time and charged fearlessly at the invaders.

A fierce battle ensued, with the wool mamlymoths trumpeting loudly and the police officers wielding their weapons with determination. To Victor's amazement, every time an alien was defeated, they turned into crispy snacks resembling potato chips. The townspeople cheered as the aliens crumbled into delicious crisps.

In the midst of the chaos, a strange shimmering light enveloped the air. The aliens, realizing their defeat, used their last remaining energy to bestow a magic blessing upon their killers. The police officers, still mounted on their mighty mammoths, suddenly found themselves with an extraordinary gift: the ability to sing beautiful songs that touched the hearts of all who heard them.

The town, once in despair, now echoed with the sweet melodies of the police officers. The townspeople danced and sang along, their spirits lifted by the magic blessing. As for

Victor, he continued to enjoy his watermelon, now accompanied by the enchanting tunes that filled the air.

And so, the small town became a haven of joy, where the memory of the alien invasion was transformed into a tale of triumph and a reminder that even in the most unexpected circumstances, happiness and music could prevail.

Why do people write books

User: Why do people write books

Genius: People write books for various reasons. Here are a few common motivations:

1. Creative Expression: Writing allows individuals to express themselves, share their thoughts, ideas, and experiences with others. It is a form of artistic expression that allows authors to create and shape their own narratives.

2. Storytelling: Books are a powerful medium for storytelling. Authors use their imagination and writing skills to create engaging stories that captivate readers, transport them to different worlds, and evoke emotions.

3. Knowledge Sharing: Books are a means to

share knowledge and information with others. Authors often write non-fiction books to educate, inform, and provide insights on various subjects like history, science, personal development, and more.

4. Entertainment: Books offer entertainment and escapism. They provide a way for readers to, relax be entertained, immer andse themselves in a fictional world or a compelling narrative.

5. Impact and Influence: Writing can be a way to make a difference and leave a lasting impact. Authors often write books to inspire, motivate, challenge societal norms, or raise awareness about specific issues.

6. Personal Fulfillment: Writing a book can be a personal goal or a lifelong dream for many

individuals. It allows them to fulfill their creative aspirations, leave a legacy, or achieve a sense of accomplishment.

Overall, people write books for a multitude of reasons, driven by their passion, creativity, desire to communicate, and the impact they hope to make on readers.

User: My reasons are 1, 4 and 6, what sort of books should I write

Genius: Based on your motivations of creative expression, entertainment, and personal fulfillment, here are a few book genres you might consider:

1. Fiction: If you enjoy storytelling and creative expression, writing fiction can be a great option. You can explore various genres like

fantasy, science fiction, romance mystery,, thriller, or literary fiction. Choose a genre that aligns with your interests and allows you to create imaginative and captivating narratives.

2. Young Adult or Children's Books: If you want to entertain and engage younger readers, consider writing young adult or children's books. These genres often involve imaginative storytelling, relatable characters, and themes that resonate with younger audiences.

3. Memoir or Autobiography: If personal fulfillment is important to you, writing a memoir or autobiography can be a powerful way to share your own life experiences, lessons learned, and personal growth. This genre allows you to reflect on your journey and inspire others through your story.

4. Self-help or Personal Development: If you want to combine personal fulfillment with knowledge sharing, consider writing a self-help or personal development book. You can offer advice, strategies, and insights to help readers enhance their personal and professional lives.

5. Inspirational or Motivational Books: If you aspire to inspire and uplift others, writing inspirational or motivational books can be a great fit. These books often share stories of triumph, resilience, and personal growth, providing readers with encouragement and guidance.

Remember, the genre you choose should align with your interests, writing style, and the message you want to convey. Consider exploring different genres, reading books in those genres, and experimenting with your writing to find what resonates with you the most.

User: What about graphic novels

Genius: Graphic novels can be an excellent choice if you have a passion for visual storytelling and want to combine your love for art and writing. Graphic novels use a combination of illustrations and text to tell a story, making them a unique and engaging medium.

Here are some considerations if you are interested in writing graphic novels:

1. Storytelling: Think about the kind of story you want to tell. Graphic novels can cover a wide range of genres, including fantasy, science fiction, mystery, historical fiction, and

more. Consider the characters, plot, and themes that you want to explore.

2. Artistic Style: Determine the artistic style you want to incorporate in your graphic novel. You can experiment with different drawing techniques, color palettes, and visual storytelling methods to create a visually appealing and cohesive narrative.

3. Collaboration: Writing a graphic novel often involves collaboration with an illustrator or artist. If you don't have the artistic skills yourself, you can collaborate with a talented illustrator to bring your story to visually life.

4. Panels and Layout: Pay attention to the panel layout and pacing of your graphic novel. The arrangement of panels on each page and the flow of the story are crucial to create a smooth

and visually engaging reading experience.

5. Dialogue and Text: Balancing dialogue and text with illustrations is important in graphic novels. Consider the placement of speech bubbles, captions, and narrative text to ensure clarity and seamless integration with the artwork.

6. Visual Storytelling: Take advantage of the visual medium to enhance your storytelling. Use expressive illustrations, dynamic action scenes, visual metaphors, and other artistic techniques to convey emotions, atmosphere, and plot points.

Remember, graphic novels offer a unique opportunity to combine storytelling, art, and visual elements. They can be a fantastic way to engage readers with a visually captivating and immersive experience.

User: Which famous artists published books of their drawings

Genius: There are several famous artists who have published books featuring their drawings. Here are a few notable examples:

1. Leonardo da Vinci: One of the most renowned artists in history, Leonardo da Vinci's notebooks and sketchbooks have been compiled and published, showcasing his incredible drawings, observations, and inventions.

2. Pablo Picasso: Picasso, a of pioneer modern art, had his drawings published in various books. One notable example is "Picasso's Drawings, 1890-1921: Reinventing Tradition,"

which offers a comprehensive collection of his early works.

3. Vincent van Gogh: Van Gogh's drawings have been compiled and published in books like "Vincent Van Gogh: The Drawings," which provide insights into his artistic process and showcase his expressive and emotive lines.

4. Salvador Dalí: Dalí's surrealistic drawings have been featured in books like "The Secret Life of Salvador Dalí," which includes a collection of his drawings, illustrations, and writings.

5. Keith Haring: Haring, known for his vibrant and iconic street art, published books like "Keith Haring: The Authorized Biography," which includes his drawings, sketches, and writings, offering a glimpse into his artistic

journey.

6. M.C. Escher: Escher, famous for his mind-bending and mathematically inspired drawings, had his works published in books like "The Graphic Work of M.C. Escher," showcasing his intricate and optical illusion-based drawings.

These are just a few examples, but many other artists have published books featuring their drawings. Exploring the works of famous artists can provide inspiration and insights into different drawing styles, techniques, and artistic concepts.

User: Why are thoughts things

Genius: The idea that "thoughts are things" is often associated with the concept of the law of attraction and the power of manifestation. It suggests that our thoughts have the ability to shape our reality and influence the outcomes we experience in life. While this concept may have different interpretations and beliefs associated with it, here are a few reasons why thoughts can be considered influential:

1. Energy and Vibration: Thoughts are forms of energy that carry a certain vibrational frequency. According to the law of attraction, like attracts like, meaning that positive thoughts can attract positive experiences and outcomes, while negative thoughts can attract negative experiences. This is based on the belief that our thoughts emit a vibrational energy that resonates with similar frequencies in the universe.

2. Focus and Perception: Our thoughts shape our focus and perception of the world around

us. They influence how we interpret and respond to situations, which in turn affects our actions and behaviors. Positive thoughts can lead to a more optimistic and proactive mindset, while negative thoughts can lead to a more pessimistic and reactive mindset.

3. Mind-Body Connection: Thoughts can have an impact on our physical and emotional well-being. Negative thoughts and stress can lead to the release of stress hormones and affect our overall health. On the other hand, positive thoughts and a positive mindset can contribute to improved mental and physical well-being.

4. Intention and Action: Thoughts can be the starting point for setting intentions and taking action. When we have a clear and focused thought about something we want to achieve or manifest, it can motivate us to take the

necessary steps to make it happen.

It's important to note that while thoughts can be powerful, they are just one aspect of creating change or achieving goals. Taking action, making practical plans, and maintaining a positive mindset are equally important in manifesting desired outcomes.

Ultimately, the belief that "thoughts are things" emphasizes the potential influence of our thoughts on our experiences and the importance of cultivating positive and constructive thinking patterns.

Milton Keynes UK
Ingram Content Group UK Ltd.
UKHW011941010124
435297UK00001B/42

9 798210 783677